For Rosie and Raffi – N.K.

STERLING CHILDREN'S BOOKS
New York

An Imprint of Sterling Publishing
387 Park Avenue South
New York, NY 10016

STERLING CHILDREN'S BOOKS and the distinctive Sterling Children's Books logo are trademarks of Sterling Publishing Co., Inc.

First published in Great Britain 2011 by
Egmont UK Limited
239 Kensington High Street
London W8 6SA

ISBN 978-1-4027-9781-1

Distributed in Canada by Sterling Publishing
c/o Canadian Manda Group, 165 Dufferin Street
Toronto, Ontario, Canada M6K 3H6

For information about custom editions, special sales, and premium and corporate purchases, please contact Sterling Special Sales at 800-805-5489 or specialsales@sterlingpublishing.com.

Manufactured in China
Lot #:
2 4 6 8 10 9 7 5 3 1
03/12

www.sterlingpublishing.com/kids

STERLING CHILDREN'S BOOKS
New York

"I'm climbing up!" said Fluff.

"I'm climbing up!" said Billy.

"I'm sliding down!" said Fluff.

"I'm sliding down!" said Billy.

"AAAAAAAAAA

"AAAAAAAA

screamed Billy.

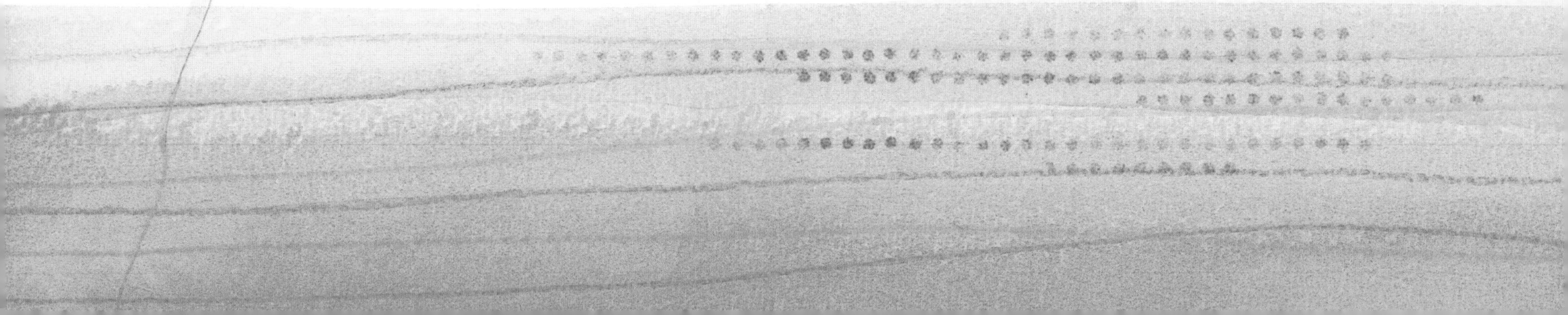

AAAAAAAHH!"

screamed Fluff.

AAAAAAAHH!"

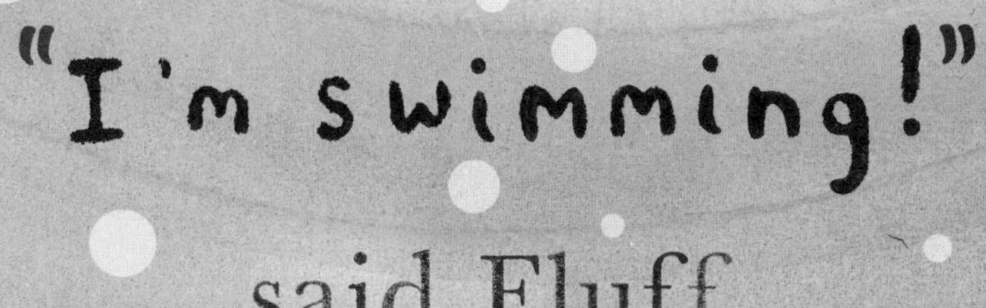

said Fluff.

"I'm swimming!"

said Billy.

"I'm splashing!"
said Fluff.

"I'm splashing!"
said Billy.

"I'm running over here!"

said Fluff.

"I'm running over here!"

said Billy.

"I'm jumping up!"

said Fluff.

"I'm jumping up!" said Billy.

"I'm rolling a snowball!"

said Fluff.

"I'm throwing a snowball!"

said Billy.

"OUCH!"

cried Fluff.

"I'm not talking to you!"

said Fluff.

"I'm not talking to you!"

said Billy.

Fluff said nothing.

Billy said
nothing.

"I'm tickling your tummy!"

said Fluff.

"I'm...
...tickling
...your
...tuh
...huh
...meee!"
laughed Billy.

HA HA

HA

HA

HA

ha ha

hee

hee

hee hee

ha

HA HA

HA HA

hee hee

HA HA

a heehee HA HA HA HA

HA HA ha ha HEE HEE

ee

A ha ha ha ha ha ha HA HA ha

EE HEE HEE

laughed Fluff and Billy...

...together!